Illustrations copyright © 1993 by Christopher Manson. All rights reserved. No part of this book may be reproduced or utilized in any form or by any means, electronic or mechanical, including photocopying, recording, or any information storage and retrieval system, without permission in writing from the publisher. Published in the United States by North-South Books Inc., New York. Published simultaneously in Great Britain, Canada, Australia, and New Zealand by North-South Books, an imprint of Nord-Süd Verlag AG, Gossau Zürich, Switzerland. Library of Congress Cataloging-in-Publication Data is available. ISBN 1-55858-192-8 (trade binding). ISBN 1-55858-193-6 (library binding). A CIP catalogue record for this book is available from The British Library. Designed by Marc Cheshire. Printed in Belgium. The text of this book has been adapted from *A Book of Nursery Songs and Rhymes*, edited by S. Baring-Gould, published by Methuen & Company, London, in 1895. The illustrations are woodcuts painted with watercolor. The type is Jenson Oldstyle.

1 3 5 7 9 10 8 6 4 2

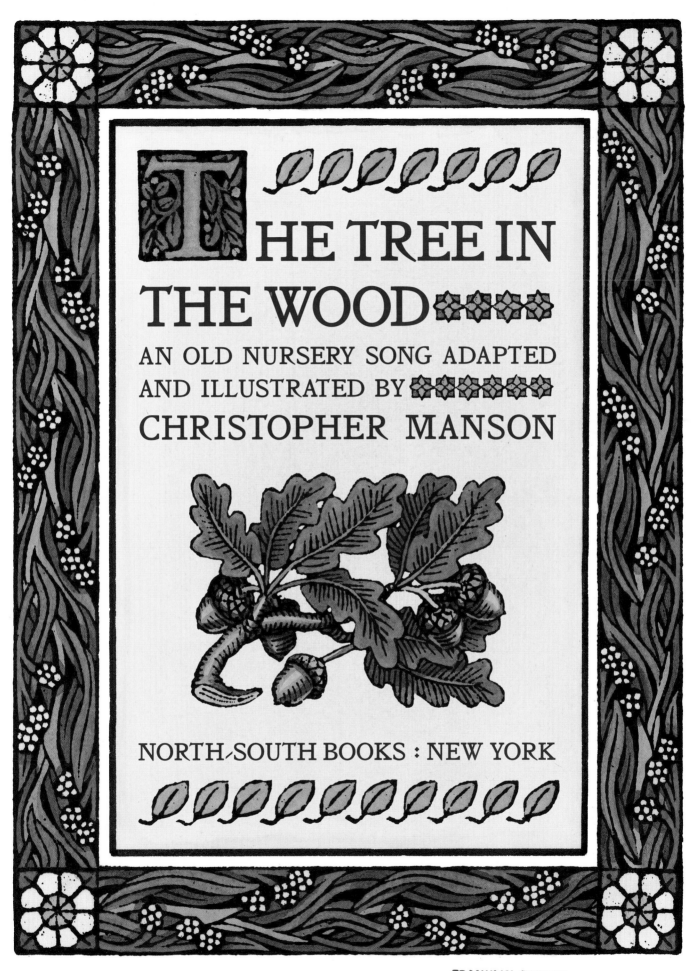

THE TREE IN THE WOOD

AN OLD NURSERY SONG ADAPTED
AND ILLUSTRATED BY ✦✦✦✦✦✦
CHRISTOPHER MANSON

NORTH-SOUTH BOOKS : NEW YORK

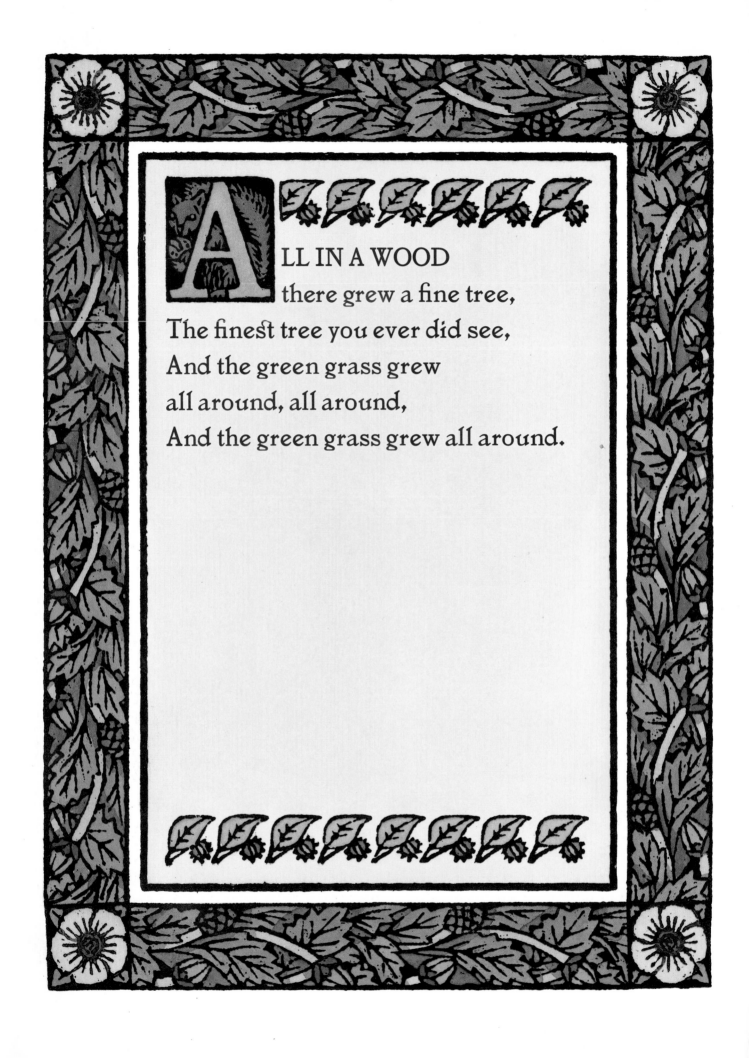

ALL IN A WOOD
there grew a fine tree,
The finest tree you ever did see,
And the green grass grew
all around, all around,
And the green grass grew all around.

THE TREE IN THE WOOD

AND ON THIS TREE
there grew a fine bough,
The finest bough you ever did see,
And the bough on the tree, and the
tree in the wood, and the green grass
grew all around, all around,
And the green grass grew all around.

THE BOUGH ON THE TREE

AND ON THIS BOUGH
there grew a fine twig,
The finest twig you ever did see,
And the twig on the bough, and the
bough on the tree, and the tree in
the wood, and the green grass grew
all around, all around,
And the green grass grew all around.

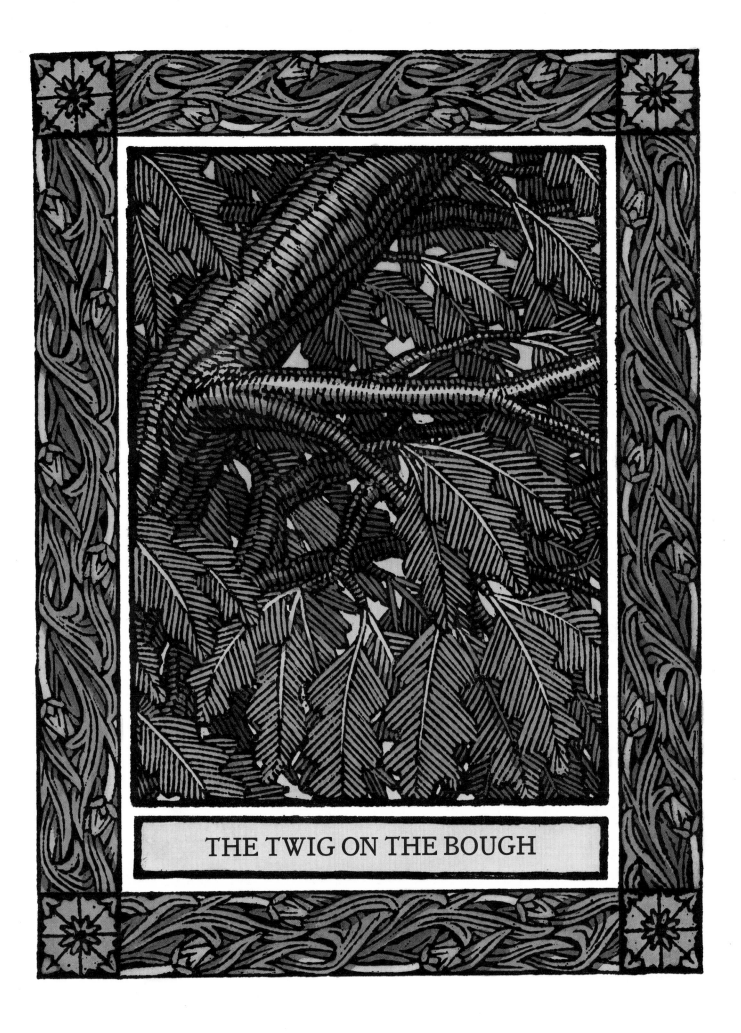

THE TWIG ON THE BOUGH

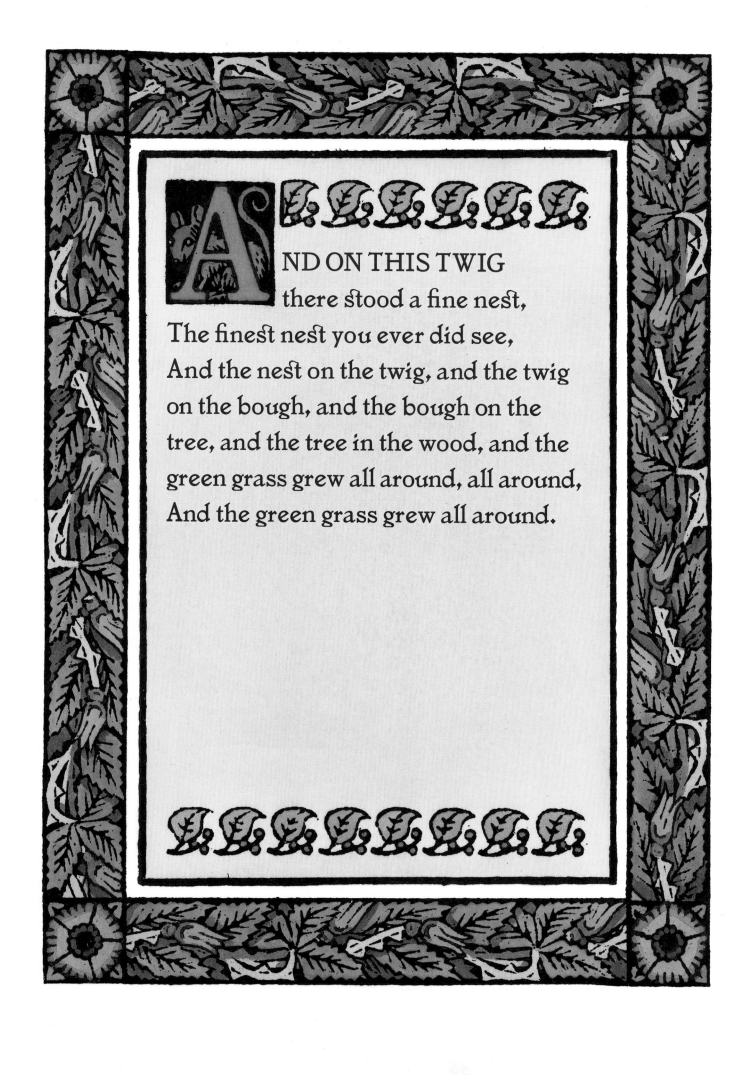

AND ON THIS TWIG
there stood a fine nest,
The finest nest you ever did see,
And the nest on the twig, and the twig
on the bough, and the bough on the
tree, and the tree in the wood, and the
green grass grew all around, all around,
And the green grass grew all around.

THE NEST ON THE TWIG

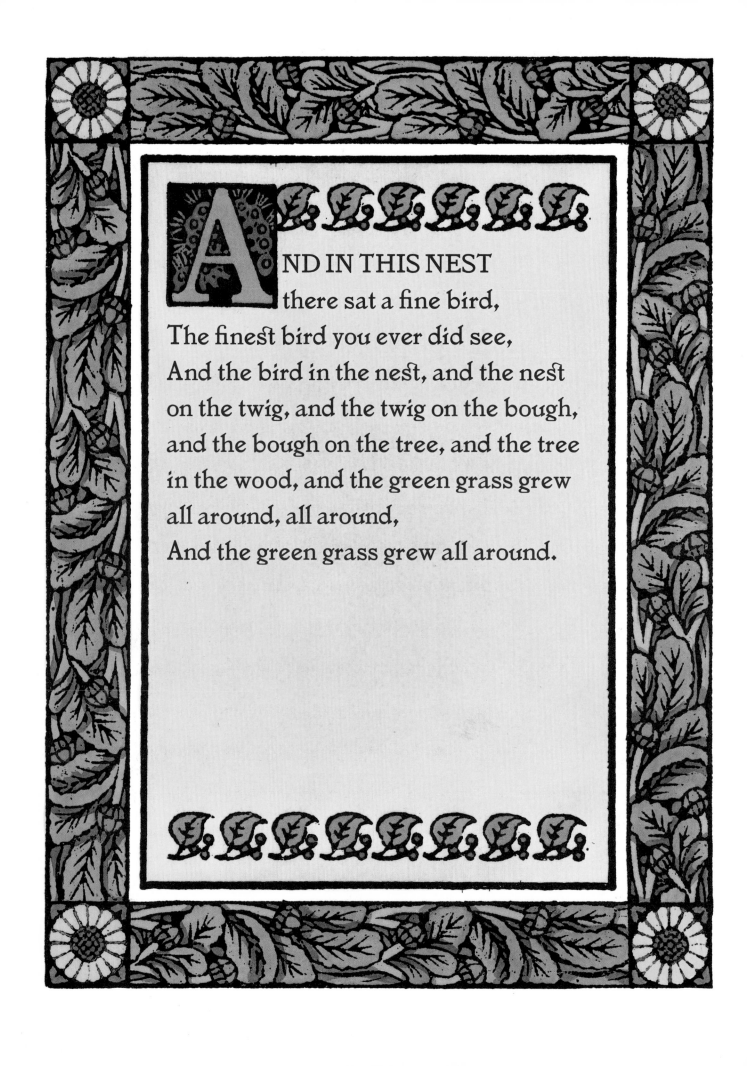

AND IN THIS NEST
there sat a fine bird,
The finest bird you ever did see,
And the bird in the nest, and the nest
on the twig, and the twig on the bough,
and the bough on the tree, and the tree
in the wood, and the green grass grew
all around, all around,
And the green grass grew all around.

THE BIRD IN THE NEST

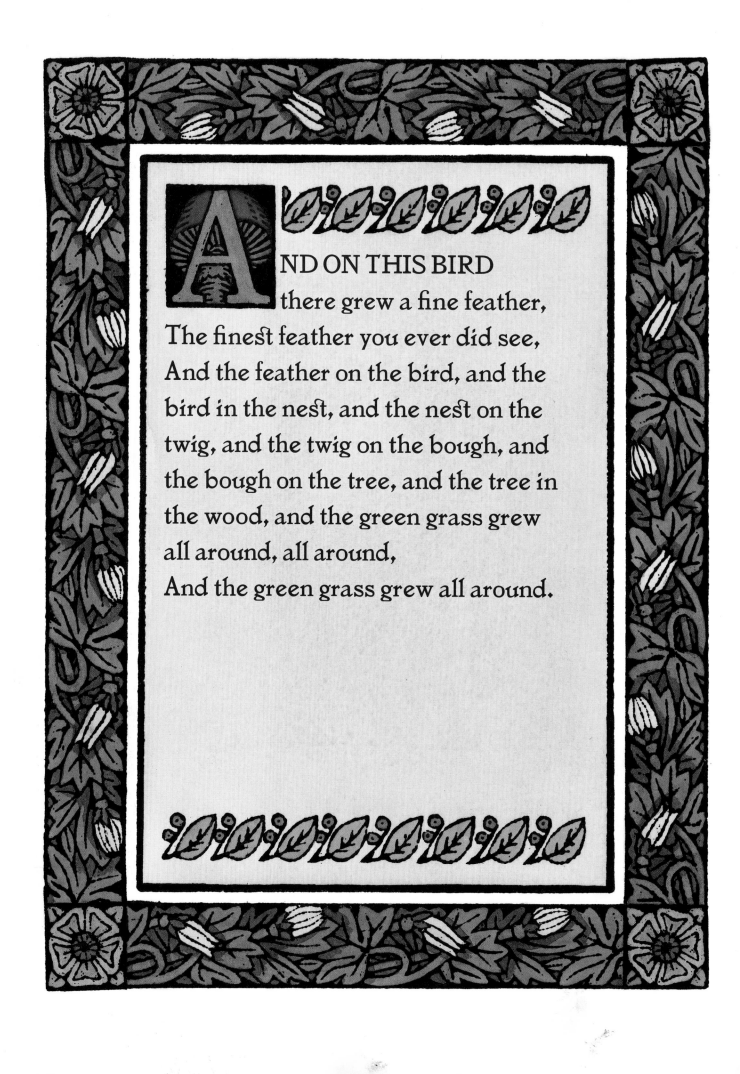

AND ON THIS BIRD
there grew a fine feather,
The finest feather you ever did see,
And the feather on the bird, and the
bird in the nest, and the nest on the
twig, and the twig on the bough, and
the bough on the tree, and the tree in
the wood, and the green grass grew
all around, all around,
And the green grass grew all around.

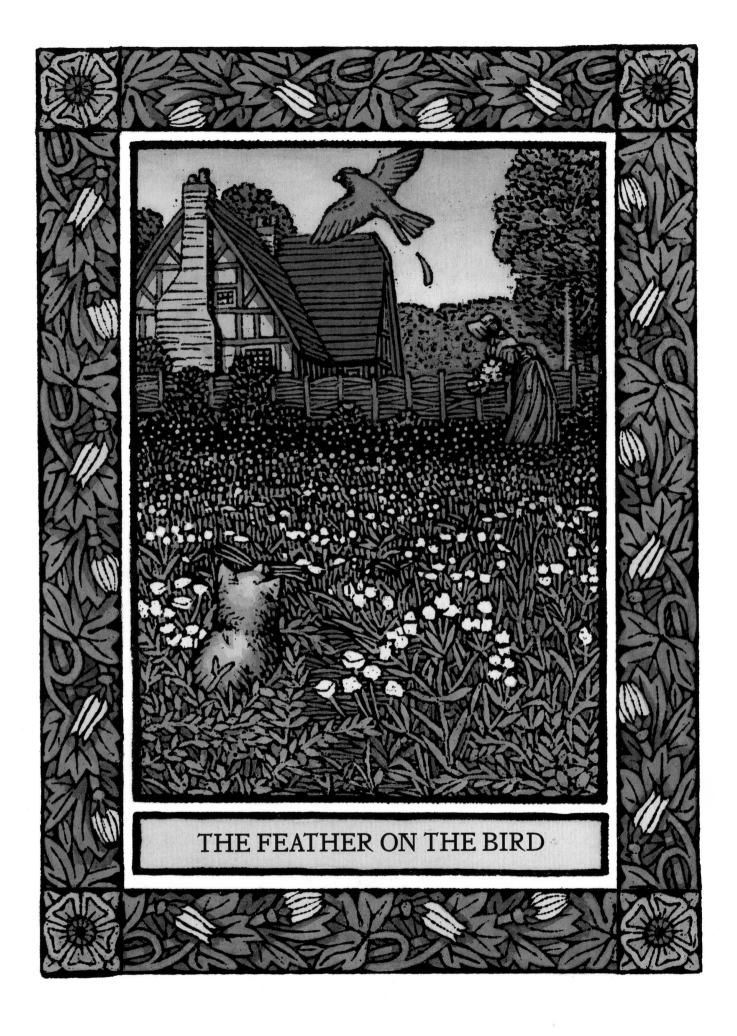

THE FEATHER ON THE BIRD

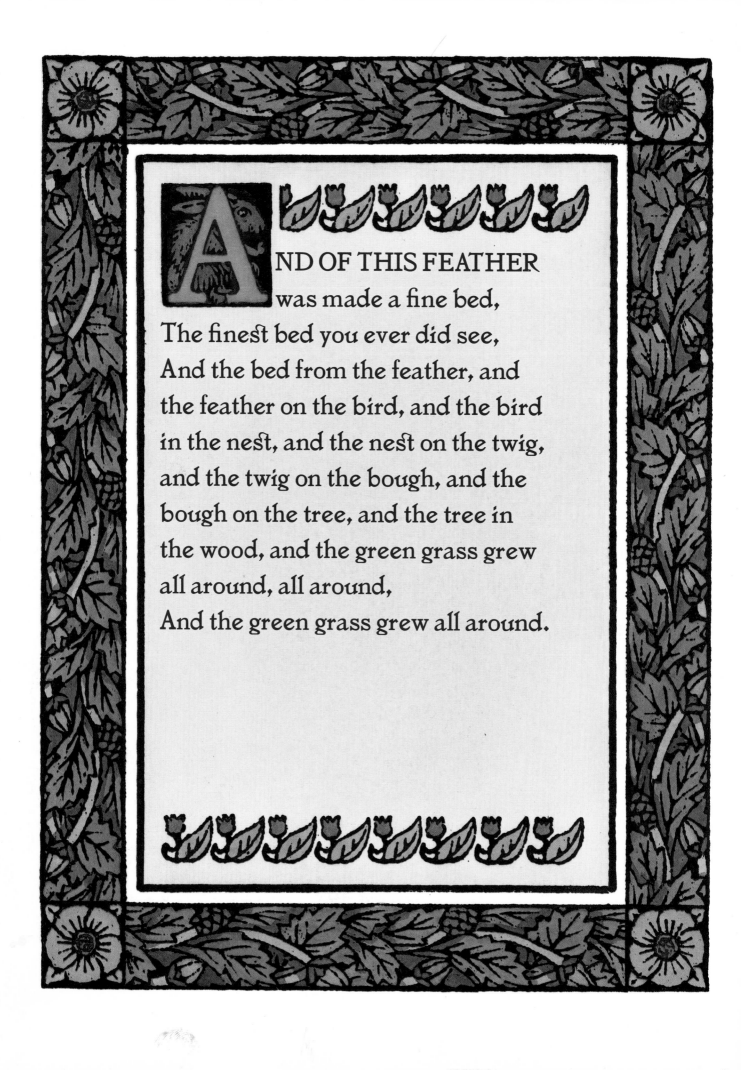

AND OF THIS FEATHER
was made a fine bed,
The finest bed you ever did see,
And the bed from the feather, and
the feather on the bird, and the bird
in the nest, and the nest on the twig,
and the twig on the bough, and the
bough on the tree, and the tree in
the wood, and the green grass grew
all around, all around,
And the green grass grew all around.

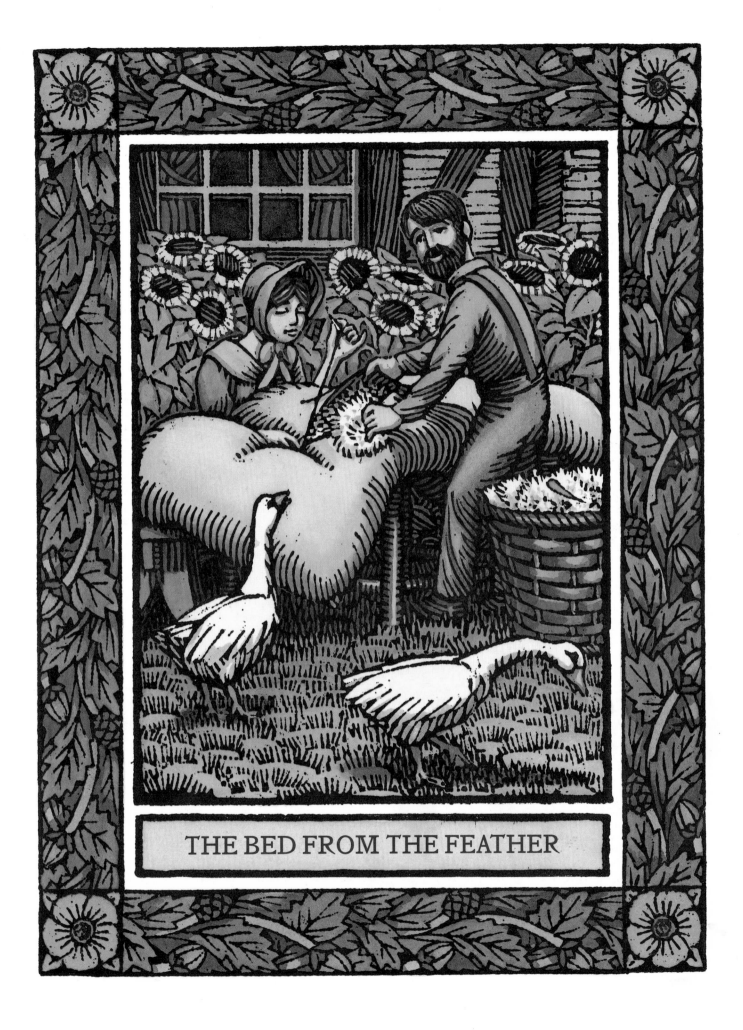

THE BED FROM THE FEATHER

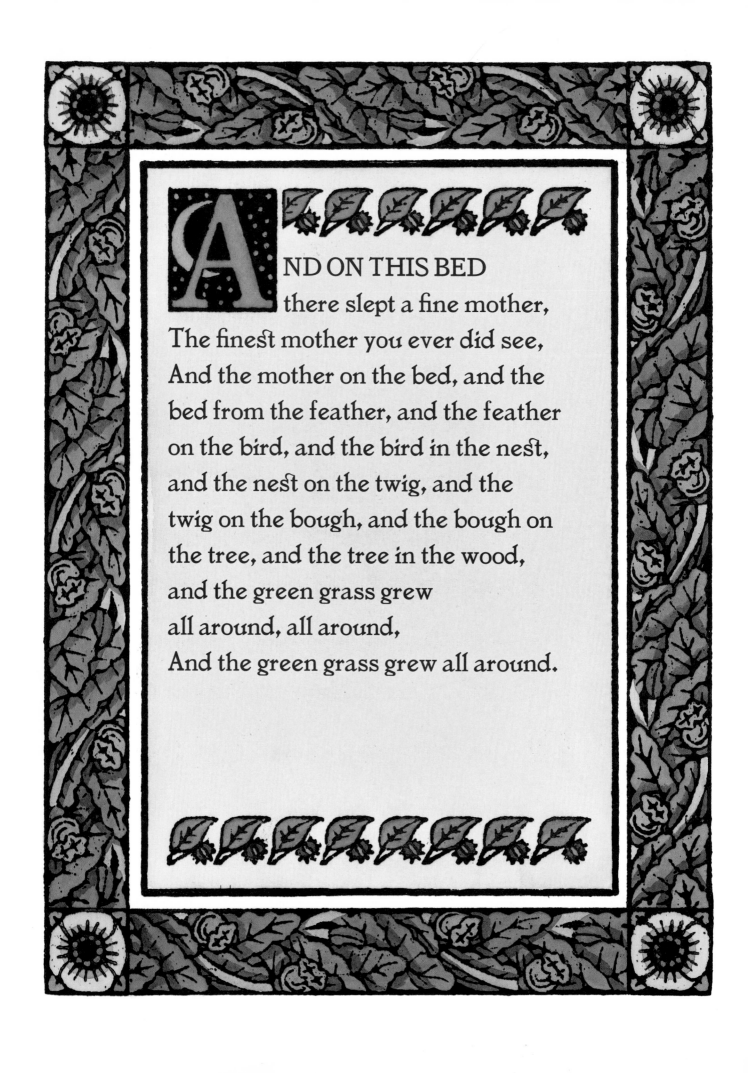

AND ON THIS BED
there slept a fine mother,
The finest mother you ever did see,
And the mother on the bed, and the
bed from the feather, and the feather
on the bird, and the bird in the nest,
and the nest on the twig, and the
twig on the bough, and the bough on
the tree, and the tree in the wood,
and the green grass grew
all around, all around,
And the green grass grew all around.

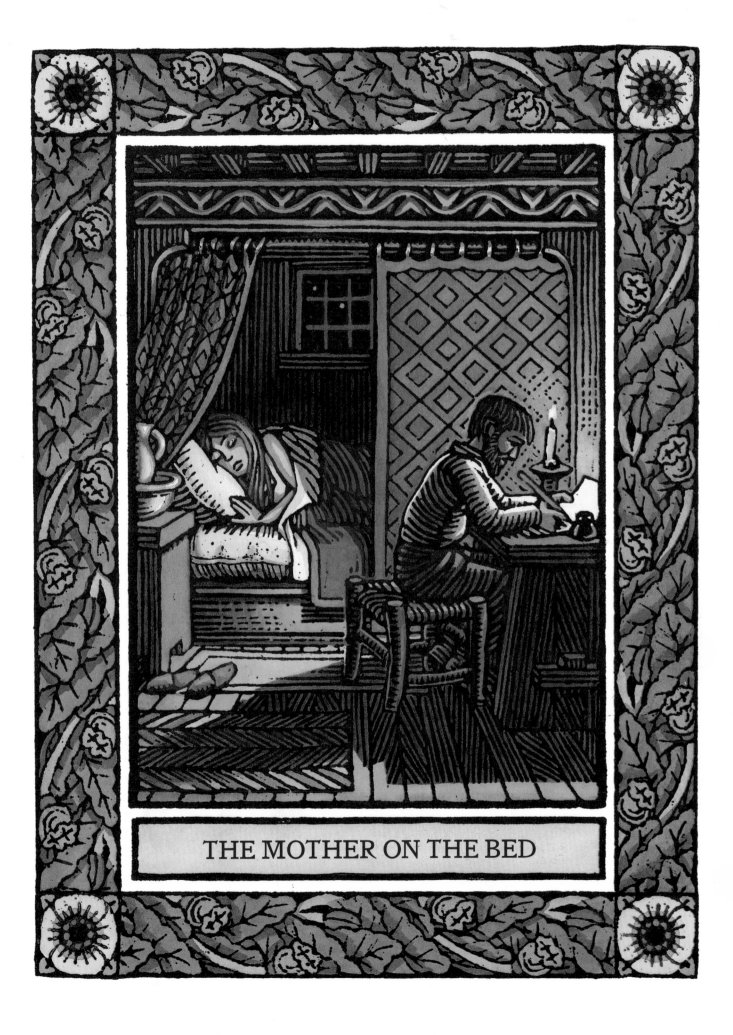

THE MOTHER ON THE BED

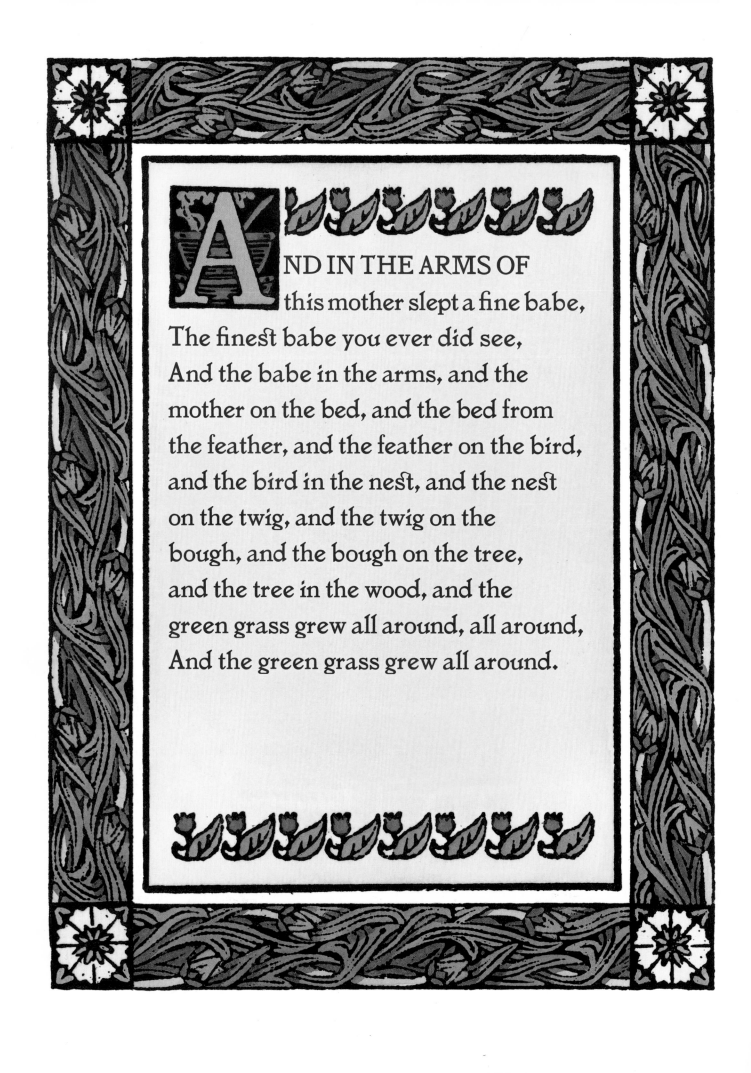

ND IN THE ARMS OF
this mother slept a fine babe,
The finest babe you ever did see,
And the babe in the arms, and the
mother on the bed, and the bed from
the feather, and the feather on the bird,
and the bird in the nest, and the nest
on the twig, and the twig on the
bough, and the bough on the tree,
and the tree in the wood, and the
green grass grew all around, all around,
And the green grass grew all around.

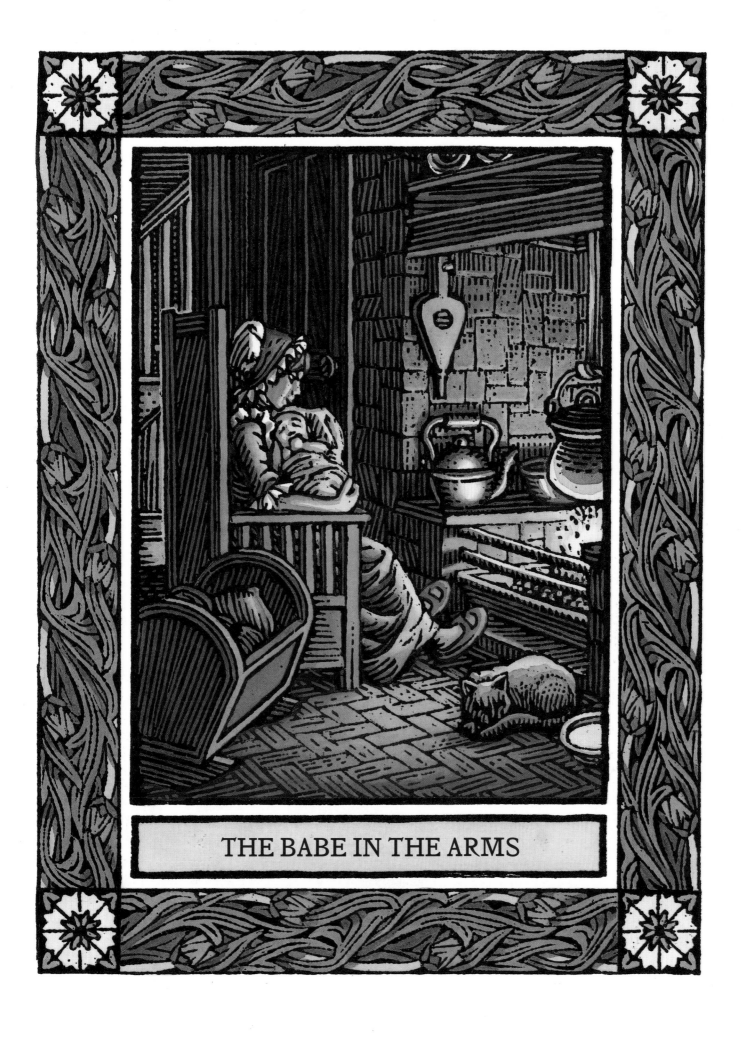

THE BABE IN THE ARMS

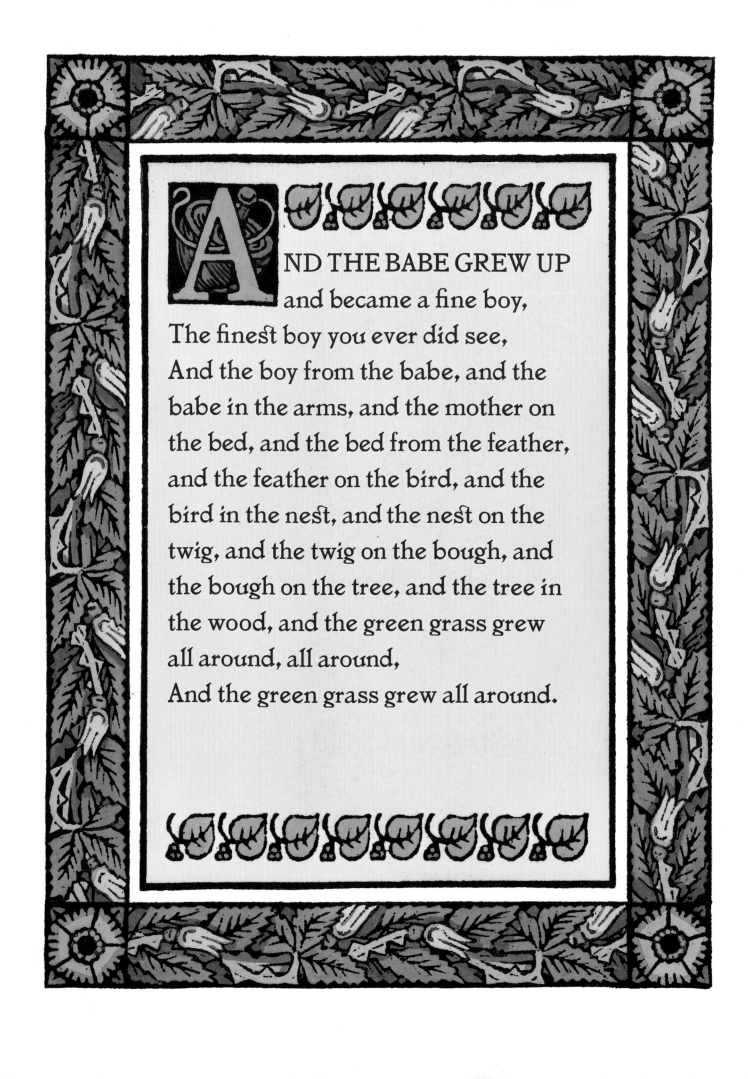

AND THE BABE GREW UP
and became a fine boy,
The finest boy you ever did see,
And the boy from the babe, and the
babe in the arms, and the mother on
the bed, and the bed from the feather,
and the feather on the bird, and the
bird in the nest, and the nest on the
twig, and the twig on the bough, and
the bough on the tree, and the tree in
the wood, and the green grass grew
all around, all around,
And the green grass grew all around.

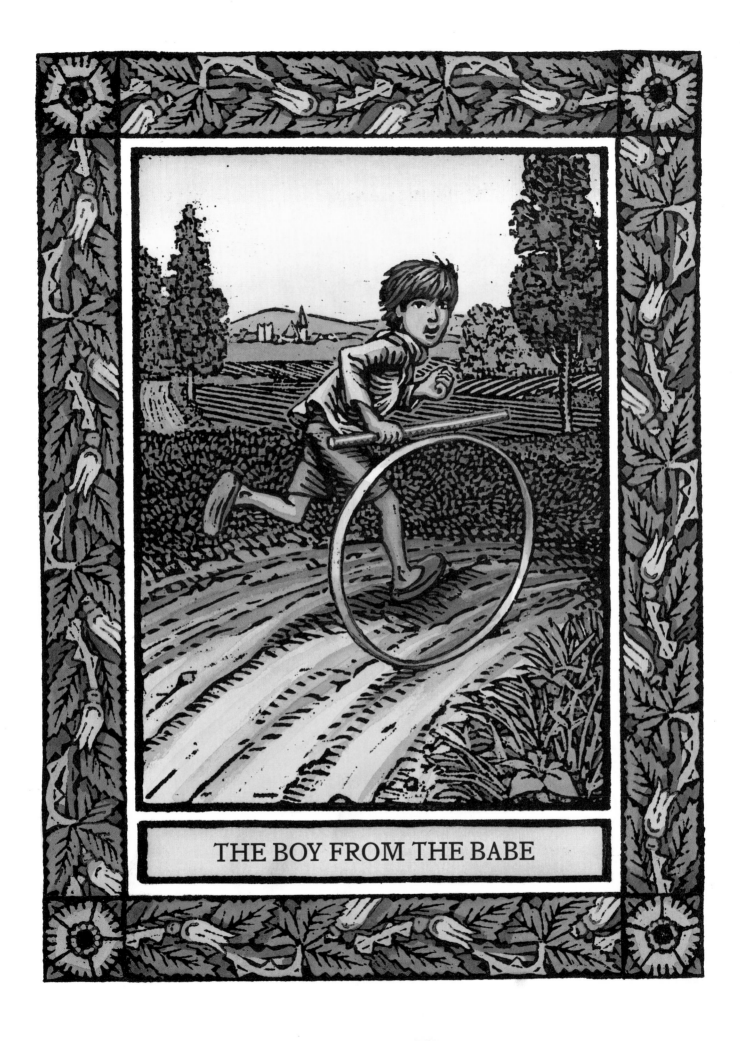

THE BOY FROM THE BABE

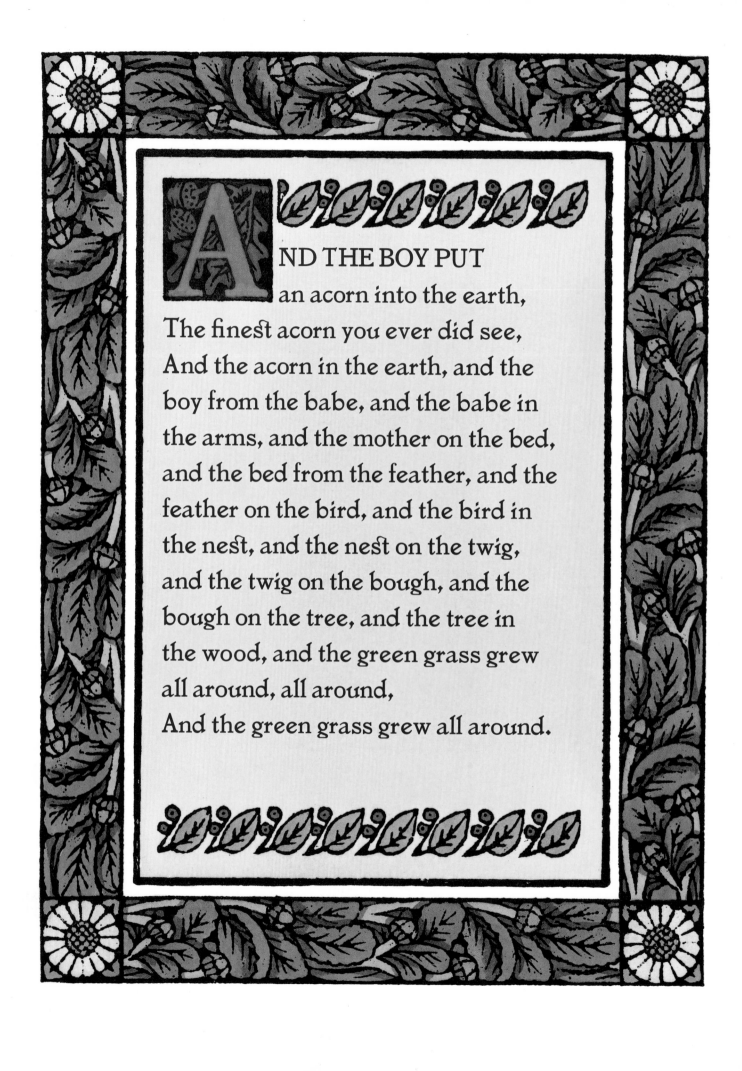

AND THE BOY PUT
an acorn into the earth,
The finest acorn you ever did see,
And the acorn in the earth, and the
boy from the babe, and the babe in
the arms, and the mother on the bed,
and the bed from the feather, and the
feather on the bird, and the bird in
the nest, and the nest on the twig,
and the twig on the bough, and the
bough on the tree, and the tree in
the wood, and the green grass grew
all around, all around,
And the green grass grew all around.

THE ACORN IN THE EARTH

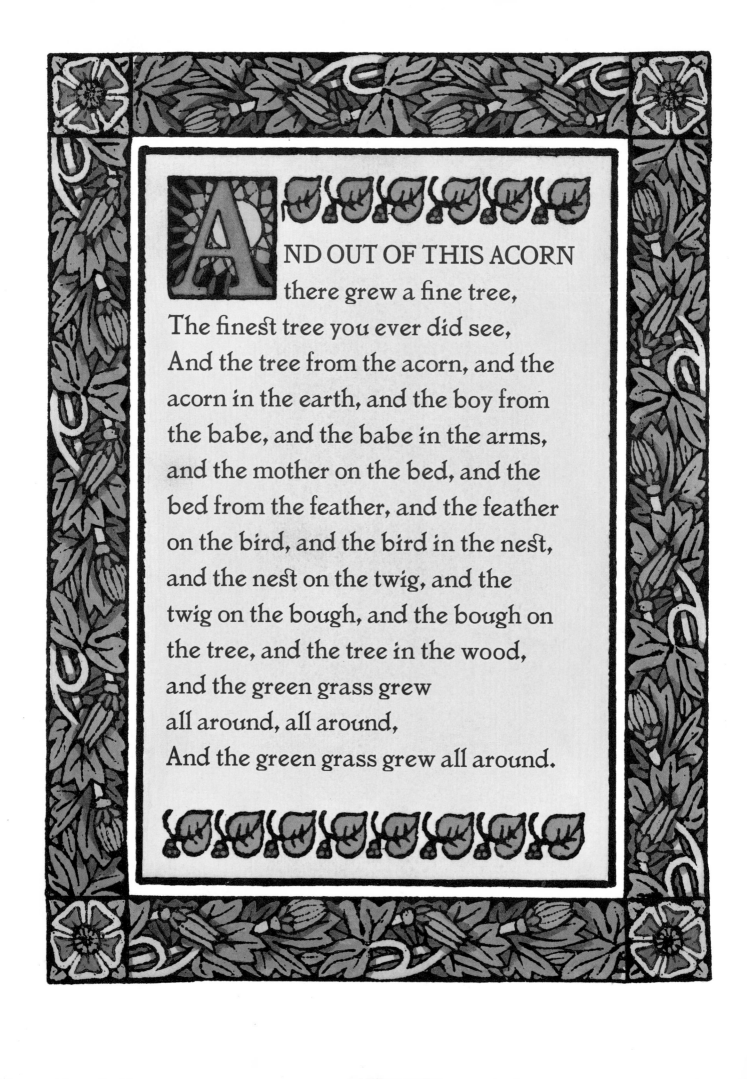

AND OUT OF THIS ACORN
there grew a fine tree,
The finest tree you ever did see,
And the tree from the acorn, and the
acorn in the earth, and the boy from
the babe, and the babe in the arms,
and the mother on the bed, and the
bed from the feather, and the feather
on the bird, and the bird in the nest,
and the nest on the twig, and the
twig on the bough, and the bough on
the tree, and the tree in the wood,
and the green grass grew
all around, all around,
And the green grass grew all around.

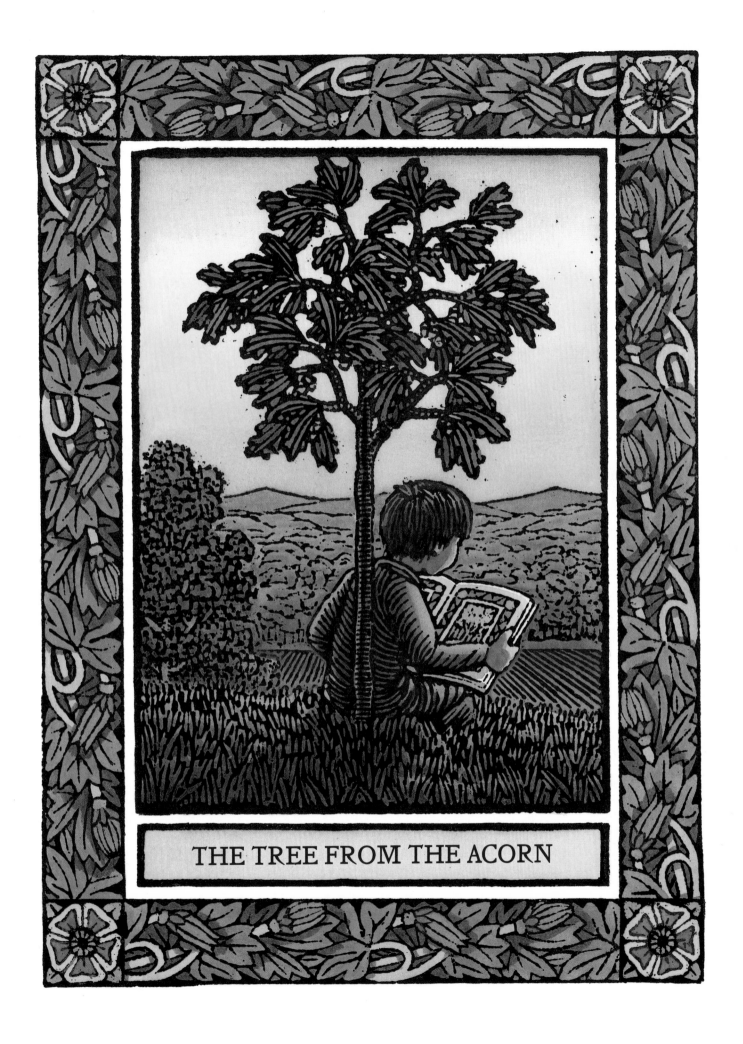

THE TREE FROM THE ACORN